MOONLIT NIGHT MUSINGS

ARUNDHATI BHATTACHARYYA

ജ

Dedicated to the ones who wear their heart

upon their sleeves ...

ജ

Contents

Contents

Part 1

Contents

PROLOGUE

ℰ

She opened her hands fully,
Never fearing again what she might lose...
The winds could blow away most of her dreams,
But the ones still left would be worth to choose...

ℰ

Your heart is the softest place on this Earth. Listen to it over all other voices around you.

--- Arundhati ---

I

Home

Don't tell me to forget my dreams,
Because you fear that I may fall;
Don't tell me the World is cruel,
To break even the strongest of all.
But tell me that even if I fail,
And my soul gets tired to roam;
I will remain safe in your heart,
I can still call it my 'Home'.

II
Somewhere Else

Some days the clock stops ticking,
Some days the time stands still;
Some days are way too different,
Some days do test your will.
Some days the moon doesn't shine,
Some days your prayer fails;
Those days with tear-stained eyes,
You wish to be somewhere else.

III
Unconditional

Give but never keep a count,
Love without the fear of a burn;
The world becomes a much better place,
When you expect nothing in turn.
You will leave with empty hands,
When your time on Earth is met;
Perhaps, that day you will know,
Life is not about what you get.

IV
Forever

In a day-dream
Broken without care,
In the whisper
Of an undone prayer;
In the scars
Which failed to heal,
In the letters
That remained in seal;
In the ignored
Pain of a tear,
"Forever" lived on
Without any fear.

V
Write

Write about how it hurt,
The lies that cut you deep;
Write about all those nights
You cried yourself to sleep;
Write about all the times
When your heart was wrong;
Write about how those days,
Somehow, made you strong.
Write them down on that page,
All your words must pour;
Write them down till nothing's left,
Then write a line more.
Write because all your tears
Were not just your own;
Somewhere, some heart needs to know
It is not alone.

VI
The Search

She travelled to places far afar,
In search of something unknown to her.
"Is it happiness for which I roam?
Or just a place to call my home?
I don't have the answer still,
But one day, I know, I surely will."
Years came and years gone,
Never, for once, did the answer dawn!
Came a day when her heart did roar,
"I don't want the answer any more.
Each of my journey has something to tell,
Till death comes, I will treasure them well."
With only a paper and a pen,
She tried to look back once again.
Patiently, she tried to focus on the past,
Every little step was revived from the rust.
Numb she sat as the answer unfurled-
To find her own self, she travelled the world!

VII

The Misfit

Had you ever seen that girl
Dancing as she broke the chains?
Had you ever heard the song
She used to sing in the rains?
Had you ever felt her words
When she wrote them on that page?
Had you ever tried to know
She longed for a home and not a cage?
She didn't belong to your world,
You never cared for a day;
You called her crazy and ignored her,
And went along in your way.
****

For years she is missing now,
The scariest thoughts are screaming loud;
Tell me she has found her home,
And hasn't become one of the crowd.

VIII

The Birth

Blank white diary,
Dark red ink;
A sleepless night,
A moistened blink.
A shooting star,
A hopeless dream;
A raging heart,
A silent scream.
A chaotic mind,
Pages were torn;
Amidst this mess,
A poet was born.

IX

IF

If Life was a fairy-tale,
With a promise of being fair;
If all dreams could become true,
And there were answers for every prayer.
If there was no heartbreak,
Never a drop of tear to shed;
If people cared enough to see,
Some could breathe even when dead.
If tomorrow could rewind the past,
And cautions came before mistakes;
If before choosing its own path,
The heart was aware of all the stakes.
If the nights were not so dark,
And the roads a little less stiff;
If the middle two letters of 'Life',
Never were that tragic 'If'.

X
New Dawn

To the dreams that died in vain,
To the tears of silent pain;
To the words we failed to say,
To the prayers that lost their way;
To the poems that searched a name,
To the bridges caught in flame;
A new dawn brings a pristine hope,
A tranquil promise, an unknown scope.
Hold the pen, the pages are new,
Make some mistakes and correct a few.
Worry not if things will mend,
Only the story stays in end.

XI
Love & Hatred

At some time long, long ago,
Love made a mistake in her pride;
"I leave marks on hearts I touch",
The joy in voice she failed to hide.
Hatred did not believe her words,
"You must prove what you say;
Touch my heart and show the world,
We are alike in one way".
Love put a hand on Hatred's heart,
And that one act doomed mankind;
The world knew in helpless pain,
They would both now turn it blind.

XII

The Mask

I watch the Moon
Glowing amidst the Stars,
Never has she feared
To display her scars.
I watch the Rose
Who says with pride,
The thorns aren't something
That she should hide.
I look at the mirror
And try to see
Where did I hide
The true real me ?

XIII
Love Was Not

Love was not the holding of hand,
Love was the grip that tightened in fear;
All our laughs, Love wasn't so grand,
Love was when you consoled my tear.
Love was not the vows we made,
Love was in the ways we cared;
Love was not the words we said,
Love was in the silence we shared.

XIV

The Words

'Those were simple words for me,
They could never cause such a hurt."
You said to cover up all the lies,
The ones I didn't doubt from start.
To know how deep words can cut,
For once, try to answer me;
How much will the stone go down,
If it's ever thrown in the Sea?

XV
Letting Go

"Hold On! Hold On!",
Shouted Hope.
"Cowards give up,
When there is scope."
Smiled Love
With tears in eyes,
Took her years
To become this wise.
The moment your heart
Tells a 'No';
Be sure, the art is
In letting go.

XVI
The Strangers

With the diary wide open,
I sat with tears in my eyes;
I would die a thousand times,
Reading it was just not wise.
"Flip the pages from the back",
Said my heart, skipping a beat;
As I finished, there was hope,
The strangers were yet to meet.

XVII

The Lesson

She spread the wings to soar amidst the cloud;
In her world of dreams, away from the crowd.
Her heart didn't need to fear at all,
It knew you were there to catch her fall.
She would never doubt her fate,
Till her feeble wings cramped under weight.
Poor crazy soul, she fell from a height;
Alas! You were nowhere there in sight.
****

Look, she flies again with broken wings;
The song of freedom is all she sings.
Her heart doesn't need to fear at all,
It knows how to rise after a fall.

XVIII

The Message

Her love was deep, they knew too well,
How much she could burn.
But shouldn't she atleast check, for once,
What she got in turn?
"Silly girl! Silly girl!
When will you learn?
Love is something that you should
Always make them earn."
Oh! The World, couldn't you hear,
The message she tried to send?
The ones giving less risk more to lose,
When everything comes to an end.

XIX

The Play

Love in eyes and knives in hands,
A well-knitted plot with a perfect drill;
They entered the Stage in crafted times,
Dressed as Saviours, they came to kill.
Her heart was stabbed from front and back,
They didn't let a chance go by;
When the final blow was struck,
They left her out in the snow to die.
Blood and cold choked her voice,
Pitilessly, they danced with glee;
The faces she had ever loved,
Used her silence as their plea.

****

Hours later after her death,
One by one, they came to her grave;
Tears in eyes and flowers in hands,
Bestowed the love she used to crave.

XX

The Butterfly

Days she spent in speechless agony,
No one seemed to care;
She remained cocooned in her pain,
They didn't bother to share.
Days later, when she arose,
Somehow they all came to mock;
"She can never be one of us!"
Fear and hatred surpassed the shock.
She smiled as she looked ahead,
Time had come to break her strings;
The Butterfly knew the world was hers,
As she happily spread her wings.

XXI

The Fairytale

In a kingdom, way too far,
Long, long ago, ruined by war;
Where the birds never came to sing,
And the church-bells stopped to ring;
Lived the Princess, out of sight,
Immersed in dreams, day and night;
Praying for her Knight to come to the land,
To listen to her words and hold her hand.
On a white horse from a fairytale,
Entered the Devil in perfect veil;
She didn't know how cruel was the game,
And fell for him as he took her name;
Hiding the knife under his gown,
He took her away, out of the town.
As he prepared to plunge her heart,
Love came between to play its part.
The Princess came and planted a kiss,
Never in life, his knife had a miss;
How his stone-heart melted that night!
The curse was gone, he hugged her tight.

XXII

The Unsaid Goodbye

As I started to talk to her,
I came to know of her past;
It was almost a decade ago,
She heard from her husband last.
Ten years ago, a letter came,
The border was under attack;
The word 'missing' invoked the fear,
But there wasn't a proof to back.
Days slowly turned to seasons,
And seasons became years;
Her mornings started with the hopes,
The nights ended in tears.
Hours passed to hear a bell,
A sudden call that never came;
Her mind tried to face the truth,
Her heart played a different game.
Dreams faded with the years,

Her hairs slowly turned grey;
Nights passed in pleading to Death,
To get delayed by one more day.
Her life got stuck in-between,
Not knowing what to do;
Moving on was not so easy,
What if he was waiting too?

"Those days did change me",
She said slowly with a sigh;
"A part of me learnt to survive,
A part of me had to die."

Silently I stood there fixed,
As she went out of sight;
As I bowed my head slowly,
For the wise who were right.

"Take a moment and say a goodbye,
Before you want to go away;
An unsaid ending is the slowest death
For the ones who wish to stay."

XXIII

The Choice

It's a story of long ago,
Of a land not known;
The Princess, as the only heir,
Adorned its golden throne.
She was just way too naïve;
Her heart was pure and kind;
Legend goes, that cost her bad;
Her trust made her blind.
The ones she believed threw her out
Of her golden land;
Alone she wept in her pain,
Nobody held her hand.
****

****

One day, by God's grace,
A Priest came passing by;
The only one to offer help
As he heard her cry.
He placed his hand upon her eyes
And mumbled a prayer slow;

What a miracle the words did,
They returned her eyes the glow!
"You chose the ones wrong for you
When you had a way,
Life always keeps a track,
And, somehow, makes us pay."
"I have lost all I had,
And you know well how;
Father, tell me what to do,
What choice I have now?"
"What you become is a call,
The choice is with you still;
The Sword that has caused your scars,
Or the Prayers that heal."

XXIV
The Answer

Why you have to feel so hurt?
Why you often need to cry?
Why can't you forget it all?
Why don't you atleast try?
They will ask these countless times,
The wise world will never know;
The ones who love with all their heart,
Die at the thought of letting go.

XXV

The Phoenix

How many times you need to fall ?
How much it must hurt ?
How many tears you have to cry
Before you seek a start ?
How many times the heart must break ?
How much you must burn ?
How many Phoenix will have to rise
For this world to learn?

XXVI

A Prayer

Since the day our eyes met,
Nothing remained the same;
Every breath that I took,
Got filled up with your name.
How your dreams became mine,
In my dream were you;
Perhaps, it all remained the same,
Yet, the world seemed new.
Loving someone more than self,
"Madness", they would call;
For me, it was a prayer though,
The purest feeling of all.

XXVII
The Promise

"Remember the time
And this place."
With tears in eyes,
She said with grace.
"Live your dreams,
Without any fear.
This heart knows
To wait, my dear.
And if you fail
Before reaching the line,
Come back with the scars,
I will call you mine."

XXVIII
Sometimes

Sometimes things are not the way
As you think they must be,
Sometimes to find yourself,
Getting lost is the key.
Sometimes you smile the best
When you wish to cry out loud,
Sometimes you feel all alone
As you stand amidst a crowd.
Sometimes you pour your heart,
Yet your love is never heard,
Sometimes you speak it all
When you do not say a word.
Sometimes you find the strength
As you start to walk away,
Sometimes you win the game
Because you choose not to play.

XXIX

The Parting

I remember it in vivid detail,
The night of Christmas Eve;
When you came to let me know,
It was time to leave.
And I whispered to your shadow,
That had started to fade,
How my heart had heard those words,
Long, long before you said.

XXX

Look Back

If on a day, hope doesn't shine,
And your heart fails to dance;
If you find the dreams have died,
And you pray for one more chance.
Think of the hurt that you caused,
Remember her on that day;
The girl that was madly in love,
The girl that once wished to stay.

XXXI
The Absence

We walked along hand-in-hand,
The first Summer of May;
Never, for once, I tried to know,
What you wished to say!
Years later, I traversed the path,
A heart broken and lone;
Even your pauses started to have
Some meanings of their own!

XXXII
Remembrance

We remember the dreams we could have saved,
The way they had to die;
We remember the words we should have said,
With tears in our eye.
We remember the bridges that got burnt,
In our ego's flame;
We remember the past in vivid details,
Once we lose the same.
We remember the ones we hurt the most,
And blame it on the fate;
We remember the hearts that wished to stay,
Only when it's late.

XXXIII

The Loss

The Sun still rose,
A new Dawn came;
For the Waves,
It was all the same.
The Earth kept spinning,
Time didn't pause;
Nature was changing,
Following its laws.
Yet for a girl,
Sitting far away;
Nothing remained the same,
Since you left that day.

XXXIV

The Karma

"It is never meant to be",
Said the sand on the Shore;
The Sea, though, didn't pay a heed,
As she loved a little more.
Every time the Waves left,
Nature heard her unsaid pain;
Far away, the Desert sand
Kept on waiting for the Rain.

XXXV

The Desert & The Rain

Cried his heart in silent scream,
The Sun was always cruel to him.
He kept on praying, but all in vain;
No heart ever would know his pain.
Took her time but as she fell,
Went away his burns like a spell.
The Rains had a way of letting him know-
Love is in the care you show.

XXXVI
The Unrequited Love

Whispered the Sea to the Shore,
"How I wished the world knew!
What all I would have done,
If I was loved like you."
Sighed the Moon from sky above,
As her heart broke in pain;
Another high tide she tried to cause,
Knowing it was all in vain.

XXXVII
The Sea & The Shore

Asked the Sea in silent pain,
"Will you never whisper my name?
Shall I always come and go?
Will it forever remain the same?"
Smiled the Shore with tears in eyes,
Took him years to become this wise.
"If I ask you, for once, to stay,
Can you forever remain that way?
How can I cause you such a scar?
Haven't I loved you the way you are?"

XXXVIII

Tell Me

Tell me that the Sun rises
Even after the darkest night.
Tell me Love doesn't die,
Even if it's out of sight.
Tell me souls can intend good,
Yet they act in wrong way.
Tell me that some need to leave,
Although they wish to stay.
Tell me that the hearts can care,
Even when they do not show.
Tell me that the depth of love
Only the good-byes get to know.
Tell me that you know today
Silence has the power to kill.
Tell me there's a part of you,
Somehow that loves me still.

XXXIX

The Words Unsaid

I wrote a letter in your name,
And asked the sky but all in vain,
She wept and wept but forgot to send,
The letter I wrote got drenched in rain.
I wrote a poem on the sand,
And hoped the wind would carry it far,
The sea couldn't stand a love so deep,
The poem I wrote got washed by her.
I wrote a note and pleaded the moon,
Behind the clouds, she hid her face,
She loved you too was all she said,
The note I sent couldn't find your trace.
I tried and tried in ways but failed,
My love searched for your soul to touch,
The heart kept alive those words unsaid,
Who knew they would weigh so much?

XL

The Wait

I saw the Desert waiting for the Rain,
Amidst all his burns, amidst all his pain.
I spotted the Flowers waiting all night,
For a glimpse of the bright Sunlight.
I found the River that didn't even know,
When she would meet the Ocean in her flow.
They all told me to trust the fate,
The truest love often lies in the wait.

XLI

Maybe

Maybe I wasn't wrong,
Maybe you meant to stay;
Maybe we could have tried,
To end it in a better way.
Maybe you were just as hurt,
Maybe silence was your scream;
Everything that happened back then,
Maybe it was all a dream.

XLII

Love & Hope

The church-walls echoed with prayers unheard,
The dreams knew they won't find any way,
The new-born leaves kept writhing in pain,
In that hot, dry summer of May.
The birds could no more sing their song,
The dying stars lost their power to give,
But as the poet wrote some words of Love,
Deep down, Hope knew it would live.

XLIII

The Farewell

I know not what lies in store,
How our story will find its end;
To save a love just this true,
All my prayers I can spend.
You will remain in my breaths,
As I sleep or stay awake;
In my veins, you will flow,
That's the only promise I make.
A soldier's life is not his own,
Do not cry, it's getting late;
Give me a kiss and let me go,
The call of duty cannot wait.
If we never meet again,
And hopes die on a cruel day;
Keep me in your heart, my love,
Forever, there I will stay.

XLIV

The Numbers

So many words they didn't say,
When life still had its way.
So many dreams were put on hold,
If only, on time, they were told!
Life is short and days are few,
Not all get a morning new.
Speak your soul when there is time,
Find your dreams, it's not a crime.
Break your heart and break your bone,
But, for God's sake, turn the stone.
Death didn't come with grace, my friend,
They all became numbers in the end.

XLV
Love Will Triumph

We will again hold our hands,
Utter the words we didn't say;
Once again, Love will triumph,
Hope will smile on that day.
The Sky will cry tears of joy,
For its Earth that conquered pain;
Two souls will find a home,
Under an umbrella, in the rain.

XLVI

Terribly Tiny Stories

Address

Years later, her unsent letters craved for an *address*.

And, so the paper-boats started the search...

৩

Alzheimer's

Sleepless nights for 25 years- Nobody ever cared.

The day she had her first sound sleep, they wanted a cure for her Alzheimer's.

৩

Asylum

Dressed in the bridal Red Choli, she stood in front of the mirror.

"Perfect", she smiled and closed her eyes to imagine his face.

The sweet fragrance of her hand-woven garland filled the asylum.

৩

Betrayal

"I thought you were just like me ", Loyalty sighed.

"So did I ", smirked *Betrayal.*

ॐ

Birthday

12:03 AM: The telephone rang

"Happy *Birthday*", came the wish.

"You are late", she feigned anger.

"Yeah... by Forty years", sighed a broken voice...

ॐ

Change

"Why will you do it ?" asked Tomorrow with tears in eyes,

"Even if you forgive, you will still remain the same."

Smiled Yesterday, *"It will change you."*

ॐ

.

Colour

Aware of her favourite *colour*, he pondered over the
birthday gift.

--- Red Dress or Red Roses ?? ---

Finally, settled for a hand-written letter.

The colour looked the best on her cheeks.

ॐ

Crayons

Red River ...

Yellow Leaves ...

Black Dove ...

As God started playing with His *Crayons*, apocalypse
doomed in.

ॐ

Crowd

We wish to get lost in the *crowd*.

We search for a face there, too.

৪৩

Diary

"Why do you even exist when I am here?" the Autobiography mocked.

"For the chapters you seem to forget", replied the *Diary*.

৪৩

Distance

As a Mathematics scholar, he always thought that *distance* was measurable ...

... till the day he saw it in her eyes...

৪৩

Favourite

She never knew how salty the last scoop of her *favourite* ice-cream tasted.

For years, she had kept it reserved for him.

৪৩

Fine

"I am Fine ..."

Hiding the wet pillow inside the cupboard, she gathered
all her strength to rehearse the words convincingly.

... Nobody asked ...

৪০

Fire

He had a stone in place of a heart.

So did she.

Love was never on the cards, they both knew.

Cupid had plans to start a *fire* by striking the stones.

৪০

Freedom

Super-Saver Offer on Round Trip - read the dialog box.

She ticked One-Way.

... Freedom came at a Price ...

৪০

Friends

As *lovers*, they fought & banged doors at each other's face.

Hours later, *best friends* found themselves ... sitting outside
in the garden under the night sky.

Twinkled the stars.

ജ

Goodbye

Once, the Gun and the Knife competed for the "Cruelest
Killer" title.

Laughed *Goodbye* at their ignorance.

ജ

Habit

The walking-stick did not help.

She trembled... she fumbled...

until he took her hand in his.

*An old habit for the last fifty years, GrandMa relied only on
GrandPa to cross the road.*

Heart

"Excuse me, Ma'am! You are leaving your Boarding Pass behind", the Attendant shouted from the Counter.

"I am sorry", she apologized.

... Can you please check for my heart as well? ...

ঁ

Holi

"Happy *Holi*", he smiled and applied the red gulal on her cheeks.

This time, she didn't blush.

Quietly, he put the picture back inside the diary.

ঁ

Home

Everyday their eyes spoke as they passed each other in two separate queues.

For some brief seconds of the day, the Concentration Camp felt like a home...

ঁ

Kindness

"Who needs you when I am here ?" asked Wisdom.

"The hearts that you have failed to heal", smiled *Kindness*.

ॐ

Lies

"I am slipping", she said softly as the rains grew heavier.

"That's why I don't like you wearing those fancy sandals", he tried to sound serious and inched closer to hold her hand.

Winked the lightning at their lies.

ॐ

Lost

She *lost* her heart.

Her poems *found* a name.

ॐ

.

Love

Had your lunch?

Reached home?

Took the medicine?

Stop working till late night.

Don't forget your umbrella.

Passing by your favourite restaurant.

... and in those simple everyday conversations, we created our own versions of "*I love you*"...

ॐ

Magic

"Why do they believe in you when I am here?" Love asked

"Maybe, you haven't been kind enough", replied Magic.

ॐ

Moon

She stared at the full *Moon*, marveled at its beauty and wondered how it would have felt like to call it her own. *Looking at her, he did the same.*

ॐ

Name

"The sound of rain-drops on window-panes- the best music to ears", he said softly.

Shaking head in disagreement, she put her ears on his chest.

"Have you ever heard a heart beating with your name ?"

ॐ

Orphan

In the Singing Competition, the *Orphan* sang the best lullaby.

ॐ

Over

Lit three cigarettes, one after another ...

This time, she didn't stop.

His heart knew *it was over.*

ॐ

Prayers

"Just because all your *Prayers* have come true", mocked the atheist, "you belive in God".

"No", she smiled, "B*ecause they haven't...*"

⊕

Promise

No fancy dates, no lavish gifts ...

He never *promised* to give her the world.

Just ensured, she had a shoulder to cry on when she needed one.

⊕

Rain

"Why do you forget your umbrella everytime ?" feigning anger, she pulled him closer under hers.

As they started walking towards home, he got completely drenched... not in *rain*, but in love.

⊕

Rain-dance

"Rain-dance ?" he winked.

With rosy cheeks, she started pushing his wheel-chair
towards the garden.

The rains grew heavy.

&

Rebel

"Count the Sheep if you can't fall asleep", Mom used to say.

She started counting the Stars, instead.

As Mom saw an artist, a *rebel* was born.

&

Salty

"Sore-throat- Today it's all yours", he smiled sadly looking
at the cone in her hand.

Her favourite ice-cream flavour tasted *salty* that day.

&

Sea

As I wrote about you on the Sand, the Waves came rapidly
and washed it away.

The Sea couldn't risk the Shore falling in love with you.

Second

A streak of lightning ... A loud cloud burst ...

Startled, she clasped his hand tight.

Both prayed for a *second* bolt.

Shore

Every time she left, the Sea used to take away a piece of
him with her ...

... Yet, the *Shore* never complained ...

*Losing himself was the only way, for him, to stay in her heart
forever.*

Silence

"We teach all universal languages, Ma'am. Which one you want to enroll for ? "

the receptionist smiled and pointed towards the catalogue.

Frantically, she searched for '*Silence*' in the course-list.

ೲ

Stay

Scored a brilliant goal in the Soccer game.

Made it his display pic in the Social Media.

"How did you get the cut on your knee ?"

One message read amidst all the compliments.

He knew she would stay.

ೲ

Time

"Diamond Ring ... Exotic Vacation ...

No, tell me what you want on your birthday", he asked.

"Your *time* ", she answered.

℘

Unknown

Deleted the contact.

Blocked in Social Media.

The heart still skipped a beat with every call from an *unknown* number.

℘

Vow

He never *vowed* to bring her the stars.

All he promised was to tell the stars about her.

℘

XLVII
Santa Claus

Another year passed... The wait was getting longer...

A doubt slowly started clouding her mind.

Did he really ever exist or was it just a myth created to lure the children?

She shrugged off the doubt immediately. Today also, she had heard those kids in the pretty dresses talking about the gifts he had given them last night. But then, how could he miss her this year as well?

For years now, she was trying her best to be good so that at-least, for once, he would also gift her something- anything would do... she just wanted to know what it felt like to receive a gift.

Suddenly, it dawned upon her. Perhaps she had done something really wrong in the past so that he might have also forgotten her just like her parents. With tears in eyes, the 9-year old orphan girl tried her best to remember; but, not a single misdeed came to her mind. Nothing so serious a crime she had committed for which people could forget her like that!

After shedding a few tear-drops, she stopped sobbing. Life had taught her the hard way that shedding tears was a wastage of time. Instead, from this year onwards, she would prepare herself, somehow, to stop waiting for him.

By then, it was clear to her that he wouldn't gift her anything in this life; so, it would do her good if she stopped believing a false dream and saved her heart from getting broken year after year.

Hunger was slowly getting the better of her. For the last couple of days, she was having high fever due to cold and, hence, had not been able to go around and search for some work that would have given her something to eat. She was living on her stock kept in the rugged bag beside her.

She slowly opened the bag. Oh! Only one piece of bread was left.

Cursing her fate, she took it out.

She would, anyhow, have to go and find some work tomorrow.

Tonight, she would have to survive on this last piece of bread only.

Suddenly, he came and sat beside her wagging his tail--- her one and only friend in this vast world.

With hungry eyes, he looked at the bread in her hands. Perhaps, he also didn't have anything to eat throughout the day. She thought for a while and then put the bread in his mouth. Happily, he licked her fingers as he ate the piece away.

On that starry Christmas night, two souls slept side-by-side on the road-side—one with a lost faith in Santa; the other having just found one.

XLVIII

The Broken-Winged Parrot

It was one of the crowded Sunday markets of Lucknow.

As soon as she stepped out of the auto-rickshaw, the mid-noon Sun greeted her with a warm, gentle smile. She immediately regretted her decision for choosing the most horrible time and day of the week for visiting the place.

"Anyways, no point in pondering over the decision now", she thought, "I will have to finish the primary research and submit the report today; only 12 hours left. The life of a MBA student is full of deadlines", she muttered to herself.

The next few hours flew by real quick as she ran across various shops on either sides of the street, selecting her target audience and gathering data for her project.

It was another normal survey-experience for her—A few were happy to co-operate, some replied curtly, some plainly refused and most had suspicious glances.

However, at the end of it all, it was a good research as she had gathered quite a few interesting data points supporting her ideas. Happily, she went to a 'Mithai' shop on a corner of the street to have something before leaving the place.

Suddenly, her eyes fell on a bird-seller sitting on the other side of the road--- a middle-aged man, dressed poorly sitting with three cages, each having a colorful parrot.

"How can someone cage such beautiful creatures? Freedom is the birth-right of an individual but people always forget that", cursing mankind for its cruelty, she crossed the road and went to the seller.

"How much for the parrots?" she asked in anger.

"100 each", he replied, "Which one do you want? They can all sing very beautifully. I will show you now", the seller enthusiastically started the sales pitch.

"No, I want you to set them free", she cut him short, "All of them".

"That's such a noble idea, Beti", the seller smiled and then paused, "But I am afraid, this one you will have to leave behind. His wings are broken and so he will not be able to fly", he pointed towards the cage in the extreme corner.

She looked at the parrot sitting quietly in the cage, looking at the sky, probably reminiscing days from the past or dreaming about a future that would never come true. His eyes had an expression she had seen in the mirror before.

Slowly she replied, "Fine, I will take him with me."

"Sure, Beti. He is such a good learner. You can teach him any song in any language and he will always oblige", the seller was clearly happy at the prospect of a sale.

"No", she paused, "I want to learn from him."

"But what can a broken-winged bird possibly teach you?" the seller asked, clearly intrigued.

"Survival", came a faint reply.

XLIX

Love

What does 'Love' look like?

Love, as strange as it may sound, doesn't have a pleasing appearance.

Love has a heart that is scarred by the knives plunged deep in it. Those knives belonged to the ones it had trusted years ago. The wounds never heal, they bleed at the slightest touch.

Love has hands that are burnt from trying to hold on to someone for far too long. If only it knew how to let go of everything that never really belonged in the first place!

Love has sunken eyes that haven't slept for days. The tears in them have dried up, the pain is still alive.

Love has grey hairs much ahead of time because it worries way too much for the ones that mean everything to it.

Love has wrinkles on the skin because nobody has ever asked to take care of its own self.

Love has an empty pocket because all it knows is how to give.

Love has a poor memory that often fails to recollect how people have treated in the past. Instead of seeking revenge, it lays down its life for the same faces... over and over again.

Because all Love has is a hope- the only thing that keeps it going amidst all the pains and heartaches. Love hopes for a better world, it hopes to keep alive the spirit of humanity beyond the boundaries of race, creed, caste and religion.

It believes in its power to create a magic- the magic of changing lives by touching the souls. No matter how many times it gets abused, deep within, it knows that it just can not give up.

Because it has heard the story of its birth.

When Gods had failed to save the world, They created Love because They knew that Love, and only Love, had the power to save the same.

L
Stuck in Time

A flight with 143 passengers takes off from London, scheduled for a different timezone.

Two lovers, out on their first date, enter a coffee shop in Lisbon, hand-in-hand.

90 heads bow down for the Namaz in a Mosque in Lahore.

A young boy at Latur puts new mud in the clay machine. He has just got his first order of the day.

A woman in a hospital at Los Angeles screams as her labor pain starts suddenly.

****

The flight traverses half the globe and reaches its destination at Lhasa.

The coffee shop gets closed. The lovers leave.

The Namaz ends.

A new vase gets displayed for sale at an exorbitant price in a famous pottery shop.

A new life is born.

****

Somewhere, in Lucknow, a poet remains seated with a blank diary in hand, trying hard to find those perfect words to soothe the heart.

Something broken still remains broken.

LI

Givers Know Not When To Stop

There was a little girl who lived years ago in a land, far, far away- the girl who was different they all knew, the girl for whom little things mattered the most, the girl who used to dance in the rain, the girl who cared way too much and loved with all her heart.

One day, she went to the flower-market with her father. It was a different world! She had never seen so many flowers in her life- some she could recognize, some she didn't even know the names. So many colors, such beautiful fragrances- she had never experienced before. Instantly, she fell in love with the beauty of the market. She wanted to have all the flowers at home.

Her father didn't pay much heed to her words initially but finally gave in to her pleading. However, he told her that it was not possible to have the entire market at home, so she should choose one plant sapling and grow the flower by herself. That would be a far enriching experience than buying flowers from the market and decorating her room with them.

She pondered for a while. The proposal was lucrative. She decided to listen to her father and chose the sapling of her favorite flower- the Rose. So what if the flower had thorns? She was always in love with the imperfect. She knew, deep in heart, perfection was fake, perfection was an illusion.

Happily, she brought the plant home. Her heart was dancing in joy. She put the plant in the corner of the garden where there was enough sunlight. But most importantly, that corner was visible from her room; so, she could keep a constant watch on the plant and see it grow in front of her eyes.

Her father taught her the basics of gardening and told her not to forget to water the plant daily. "That will help the flowers bloom faster", he said.

She obeyed as she was told.

Her happiness knew no bounds. She started wondering when the first flower would bloom in her plant. Would it look like a real rose that she had seen in the market? Would it smell just the same? Oh! how she would show it to the world once it bloomed- it would be hers, entirely hers. That night, she even dreamt of her plant bearing its first flower. She saw her screaming at the top of her voice in joy. It was one of the most beautiful dreams she ever had in her life. She never intended to wake up from her dream.

****

The next morning, the plant died.
They said, she over-watered.

LII

The Blackhole... Where Time Stops Forever

My teacher had once said that a person would always be either a Maths person or an Arts person.

I was in Second standard then.

Took me years to realise the truth behind those words.

10th April, 2019- the first ever photo of Blackhole got published. The media went crazy and everywhere people started talking about it.

Being a Science person, naturally, you got quite excited about the news; and deep down, somewhere, I sighed that our entire evening conversation would now revolve around this topic.

I was never so interested in Blackholes and had never spent time in my life to research on them.

So as you asked me if I knew how Blackholes get formed or how they collapse, of course, I didn't have an answer.

And thus, started your knowledge transfer session to a poor soul who was not as enthusiastic as you about this entire episode!

Still I would say, initially your words were quite interesting- how Blackholes raised questions about the nature of space and time and ultimately about our existence. But then, soon my mind started to divert in other thoughts.

Perhaps, my disinterest was evident on my face and you paused.

"Are you getting bored?" you asked with a sense of disappointment in your voice.

"Not really", I lied so as not to hurt your feelings.

You sensed the same as you said, "Ok it's enough for now. Actually, I get very excited to think about the fact that there is some place in this Universe where Time stands still. Imagine what a Magic that is!"

A bright smile lit across my face as I heard those words. It took you by surprise but you didn't ask anything.

As you left the room with your eyes glued on your mobile screen reading the latest update on the topic, I silently picked up my pen and opened my diary.

Today's entry will be special.

"Human life is fragile and unpredictable", I wrote, *"but in my lifetime, I have finally found the place to love you where Time stops forever."*

LIII

Time Stood Still

A year later, he called again. It was time to return some of her belongings.

Both agreed to come to their favorite hangout joint for one last time- the CCD beside the lake where they had first met.

He arrived on time with the parcel in hand. There was no sight of her.

He sat at their favorite corner and ordered a cup of coffee.

Memories came flashing back in front of his eyes. A drop of tear blurred his vision.

Ignoring the same, he tried to concentrate on the coffee. He knew he needed to be strong in front of her.

As he was almost finishing the second cup, she entered the café.

Dressed in his favorite golden top, she was looking like an angel.

He got up from the chair to keep the meeting short.

"As usual late", he said keeping a straight face.

"Sorry", she gave her prettiest smile and all he could do was stare at the dimple in her cheeks that had once made him fall for her.

"For how long are you waiting?" she asked innocently.

Startled, he looked at his watch.

It had stopped.

History repeated years later.

Yet again at the same place, Time stood still for him.

LIV

The Timezone

I was not good in Geography.

I hated the subject with all my heart- particularly, those long boring periods where the teacher used to ask us to calculate the local time of a particular place.

I could never figure out what difference would it make to me if London was 5 hours behind us.

Yes, I was too young then to realise how important timezones are in our lives.

Life is always the best teacher and no school textbook can ever impart the knowledge that Life gives us in due course of time.

So it took me years to learn.

****

I still remember the last time I saw you at the airport, beaming in joy with the offer letter from your dream company in hand.

It was a day I would never forget in my entire life- the day when my heart was trying its best to be happy for your success, yet deep down, there was a selfish sadness that was engulfing it in every breath that I was taking. However, you were too busy that day to notice it.

"When will you reach Japan?" was all that I had managed to ask before you bade the final goodbye, after gathering all my strength to hide my tears.

"10 hours from now", you replied and then paused, "but Japan timezone is 3 hours ahead of India."

Those last few words hit me hard and the timezone calculations which I had once ignored, somehow, seemed to mock.

"Good, you will remain in my future", I said softly.

"And you will always stay in his past", roared back my heart.

... Life winked...

LV

The Loss

She sat quietly by the window as it started raining, humming a sad tune slowly. It was a sight to behold - she looked magical as I stared in awe at her dark black curls that fluttered in the wind, covering half of her face.

Beside her, she kept the empty cage where once her closest friend used to live - the white-winged cockatiel.

I had been a witness to their closeness for years.

In fact, there was a time when I used to get jealous of her fondness for that tiny creature. I had always failed to understand her love for him - so pure, so true, never expecting a thing in return. Maybe, that's what love was always supposed to be.

But, a few months ago, as I came back home one day, I found the cage empty. When I asked her about him, she just replied that she had let him fly away because it was selfish of her to keep him caged when clearly he didn't want to stay.

We never spoke about it again but I would always remember the pain that I saw in her eyes that night.

****

She paused her tune and slowly turned towards the empty cage. Even though the cage had been empty for months now, she would never forget to clean it up as a routine every day. I wanted to tell her sometimes that there was no use of it anymore but every time would stop at the very last moment.

She put her left hand upon the cage and took a deep breath.

"I miss him", she murmured slowly, "Why was he so selfish?"

I had never seen her so vulnerable like this.

I didn't know what to say.

Still to console her, I replied, "Forget it, dear. He had always wanted to fly. I won't say you did a wrong thing by letting him go", and then I paused, "but yes, I agree he was very close to you. So, in that way, I feel for your loss."

She nodded in disagreement and looked up.

"It is not a loss", she replied sternly. The strength in her voice was unmissable.

"If you ever lose someone for loving way too much, it's never your loss to begin with", she said as a drop of tear glittered in those dark brown eyes.

LVI
The Old Lady &
The Stars

Somewhere, in the distant land, where the blue sky meets the sea, there lives an old lady who keeps on spinning the wheel day and night.

Her hairs are grey, her skin is wrinkled, yet, her fingers still know how to create magic as she keeps on weaving new clothes that keep changing the colors of the sky and the ocean at different intervals of time.

She isn't visible to the human eye and, as she weaves, the lonely lady sings a song that only the wind can hear.

Only there are some nights in a year when she stops weaving and comes out in her balcony.

She looks up at the sky and talks to the stars of a long-lost past where she had met the love of her life.

The stars ask in details but she smiles sheepishly.

Age has taken a toll on her.

She has forgotten how he looked, the color of his eyes, the sound of his voice, the scent of his perfume.

Yet, she remembers in vivid details how he used to make her feel. She speaks of the ways her heart kept beating every time their eyes met, the ways her body shivered everytime their fingers crossed, the ways her breath stopped everytime he took her name.

And the stars listen in rapt silence as the waves keep splashing against the shore.

Time, however, ticks away even as the nature gets engrossed with her story.

The first rays of the morning sun appear in the Eastern horizon.

The old lady hurriedly gets up from her wooden chair and goes inside to start weaving yet again.

"Oops!" whisper some of the stars realising that they forgot to fall the previous night to fulfill a wish.

****

So, on nights when you look up at the dark sky and fail to find a single Shooting Star, remember there's a lonely heart far, far away who is whispering a story of love to them- who needs the stars much more than you on that night to pour out the contents of its heart, who wants the stars to listen to a story that will, otherwise, get forever lost in the wheels of time.

LVII

Love In The Time Of War

It was the Summer of 1943.

An attractive young man, in suits, entered a café in a small town in Lithuania.

The moment he entered, his eyes fell on the calendar hanging above the reception. All the past dates of the year were struck off in red. He started to wonder why somebody would diligently take out time for such a meaningless activity.

"Excuse me Sir, would you like to have a seat?" a voice from behind interrupted his thoughts.

He turned around abruptly.

Standing in front of him, was a young girl, in her early twenties, dressed in an orange gown with a beautiful smile on her face. Her kohled eyes were deep enough to house an ocean, her curly golden hairs were fluttering in the air, the sweet smell of her perfume was filling up the café. She was wearing heels to cover up for her short height, yet what was standing tall was her personality.

There was something in her that was far more appealing than her looks, something that was speaking of her inner strength, something that was creating an aura of mystery around her, something that told him the moment he saw her that he had never met someone like her before and it would take him long to forget her.

"Yes, of course", he smiled as he gathered himself back.

She flashed her beautiful smile and signaled him to follow her towards an empty table at the corner of the café beside the glass window. She handed him the menu card and went to the next table to take the order.

He knew he was behaving oddly and was trying his best, yet, he was not being able to take his eyes off her. The busy road outside the window, the newspaper on the table citing the daily horrors of the World War 2— everything failed to catch his attention.

After a few minutes, she again came back to his table with a smile on her face, "What would you like to order, Sir?"

The menu card was still not opened, and he didn't know what to say.

However, he managed himself well and said, "I want to try the special dish of this café."

She went away with the menu; and after around fifteen minutes, returned with a bowl of bacon salad and a hot cappuccino. "Try these, Sir", she smiled and put the food in front of him as she went back to the reception.

He didn't know how the food tasted, he didn't even know how the next one hour flew by because for the entire time, his eyes stayed glued on her.

For the next three months, it became a daily routine for him to visit the café during those early breakfast hours just to get a glimpse of her. He would always select that corner seat from where the reception would be clearly visible and would spend an hour simply by watching her busy in her work.

Perhaps, she also sensed something, yet she never said anything to him.

He could be wrong; however, he had a gradual feeling that she, too, had started to like his presence in her cafe.

He never missed to notice everyday how the past dates had been struck off without fail with a red ink on the calendar and he wondered why. Once he even asked her the reason for the same, but she didn't answer and just gave a smile.

Came one day when he was called to join the War.

As usual, he came to the café that morning and sat at his favorite spot.

However, unlike other days, his mind was full of uncertainties. There was an unknown pain in his heart and he didn't know the reason of it.

Shouldn't he feel proud that he had been chosen to fight for his motherland? Shouldn't he boast to all his fellow countrymen that it would be an honor to die for his country? But then, why his chest was feeling so heavy? Was it because he knew, deep within, that he would miss these morning hours, he would miss this café and, most importantly, he would miss her?

"Are you not well, Sir?" the sudden question brought him back to the present.

She was standing in front of him with concern in her eyes.

"Not really", he paused for a moment and then continued, "I am going to join the War".

Her face grew dark for a brief second, but she gathered herself well.

Suddenly, he lost control on his words and abruptly spoke out, "I will be leaving tomorrow morning. Will you like to come out with me for dinner tonight?"

Startled, she looked away towards the busy road. After few moments, she looked back in his eyes and curtly replied, "I am busy tonight, Sir".

There was a deep pain in her eyes and her voice was remorse and she started to leave. It was driving him crazy and he pulled her back towards him as he spoke, "Don't you understand why I come here every morning? Why are you pretending to be so heartless? I don't know if we will ever meet again. Let me tell you the truth today as I leave. I will be missing this country terribly but more than that, I will be missing you."

She kept looking towards the floor and after few minutes, simply asked without any sign of remorse in her voice, "Why? Why will you be missing me, Sir?"

This was too much for him to bear. The pain of separation was already deep in his heart, and he couldn't take any further. He pushed her away, didn't say a word anymore and went towards the door with a promise of never returning to the café again in his life.

The coming days were terrible for him.

He saw the horrors of the War right in front of his eyes, he realized how cruel human beings could become in pursuit of power, how terribly technology can be misused for selfish benefits.

Yet, what hurt him the most and killed him everyday was the thought of her. No matter what he had promised that day before leaving, all his mornings started with the prayer of returning to her. How he wished the war to get over soon so that he could get one glimpse of her!

He started to strike off the calendar dates each day without fail with the simple hope that all this suffering would end soon. Somehow, this apparently meaningless activity helped to lessen the pain of his wait. Somehow, it conveyed to him every morning that the length of the period of their separation had now become shortened by a day.

Two years passed by. Ended the War as the world sighed in relief.

The soldiers were asked to go back to their countries. They were being treated as no less than heroes. His heart was fluttering in joy. All he was wishing was to go back to the café, to go back to her. Instead of striking off the calendar date, he put a heart sign beside it and packed the calendar in his bag.

It was a Sunday evening when he again entered the café.

It was the closing time and the customers had already left. She was sitting at the reception counting the cash. She still looked the same, the only difference was the new spectacles that covered her kohled eyes and made her look a little aged.

"Sorry, we are closed for the day", she said without looking up, as she heard the door being opened; and then she saw him.

For a moment, there was disbelief in her eyes and then there were tears rolling down her cheeks.

She came running towards him, apparently for a hug, but checked herself at the very last moment.

"I never thought I would see you again", he said softly with a mix of pain and joy in his voice.

Her tears were still coming down, yet she managed to speak, "Neither did I, Sir. I can't tell you how happy I am today. You have proved them all wrong. You are the proof that people do return from the War." Her voice was painfully ecstatic!

Neither of them spoke any further. They didn't know how long they stayed like that, looking into each other's eyes as both cried their hearts out.

After some time, when he finally got back to his senses, he said, "I just came to see you tonight. Lucky me the café was still open. I will come again tomorrow morning."

Controlling her sobs, she asked, "Why? Why will you come back, Sir?"

He didn't answer and went towards the door.

Just before stepping out, he turned back and looked at the calendar hanging above the reception. All the previous dates of the calendar had been struck off with the red ink.

Holding the door in his hand, he pointed towards the calendar.

With empathy in his voice, he uttered softly,

...*"Because in your café, love knows to wait"*...